Appleblossom

Appleblossom

BY

Shulamith Levey Oppenheim

PICTURES BY

Joanna Yardley

Harcourt Brace Jovanovich, Publishers

SAN DIEGO   NEW YORK   LONDON

HBJ

A short story version of *Appleblossom* previously appeared
in *The Scribner Anthology for Young People*, in 1976.

Library of Congress Cataloging-in-Publication Data
Oppenheim, Shulamith Levey.
Appleblossom/by Shulamith Levey Oppenheim;
pictures by Joanna Yardley. — 1st ed.
p.   cm.
Summary: With the help of Appleblossom, the talking cat,
eight-year-old Naphtali comes up with a plan, involving
traditional rituals at the Passover seder, to convince
his father that a cat is just what the family needs.
ISBN 0-15-203750-0
[1. Cats — Fiction. 2. Passover — Fiction. 3. Jews — Fiction.]
I. Yardley, Joanna, ill. II. Title. III. Title: Apple blossom.
PZ7.0618AP   1991
[Fic] — dc20   89-24575

First edition
A B C D E

For Felix,
with love, and with gratitude
for never having said,
"No! No cats."
— S. L. O.

With thanks to Jane Yolen,
who opened the door for me.
— J. Y.

Ever since Moses led the children of Israel from slavery in Egypt to freedom and the Promised Land, Jews all over the world remember the event with a special spring holiday called Passover. At the Passover meal, the Seder, they give thanks to God and offer prayers for the freedom of people everywhere. They also set a special place at the table for the prophet Elijah and welcome him in by opening the front door.

Appleblossom

One bright-washed day in late April, less than a week before Passover, eight-year-old Naphtali Ha-Levi came skipping along the cobblestone street toward the synagogue. His long fair hair covered his ears. He wore a yoked school smock with long sleeves over short pants and a white shirt.

The small village in which Naphtali lived was bordered by open country. As he skipped along he could see the expanse of meadow stopped short by the great forest and the cultivated plots of the peasants in all shades of green. The pear, the apricot, and the apple trees were blooming everywhere.

"There is nothing so sweet as the scent of appleblossoms," his mother had said at breakfast that morning.

"Except the blossoms themselves." Naphtali's father had taken her hand and smiled.

Naphtali knew exactly what his father was saying. His mother was as sweet as an appleblossom. And he agreed. But as apples were his favorite fruit, he added, "And Papa, don't forget the apples."

Then his parents had kissed him. This made Naphtali happy, for his father could often be very, very stern. That was why his father's infrequent smile always made Naphtali feel just a little bit like he did when he'd been running — lightheaded and slightly out of breath. Naphtali loved that smile, so broad when it was suddenly there. And his father's laughter, even less frequent, deep in his chest.

Naphtali skipped all the way to the side door of the synagogue, where he studied Hebrew four days a week with twenty other boys.

The door was locked.

"I'm early," he said aloud, with a great rush of pleasure. The village schoolteacher had let his class out ahead of time.

Naphtali skipped on to the back of the building and across a narrow swinging bridge. The water rushing beneath was almost white. He took the path that led toward a cluster of flowering apple trees.

"I'll sit here. Then I'll be able to see the others coming."

A few more skips brought Naphtali to the first tree — low-spreading, knotted, and in full bloom.

He sat down and put his books beside him. Then he drew in a long, deep breath. His mother was right. There was no scent sweeter than appleblossoms. Just as he was letting his breath out, he heard a soft thud behind him.

Peering round the knotted trunk he saw a cat — a bit more than a kitten though not fully grown. Three months perhaps. A calico cat — white, gray, and apricot. More thin than fat — far, far more thin than fat.

"A cat!" Naphtali was on his knees beside the creature.

"A boy," the cat meowed matter-of-factly.

"Yes, I am," answered Naphtali, not at all surprised to hear the cat speak. After all, didn't animals talk in the Bible and in the tales his mother and father read to him at bedtime? "My name is — "

"I know your name."

The cat sniffed the leather thong around Naphtali's books, rubbed its chin on the top volume, then came back to Naphtali and stropped his right leg.

"Do *you* have a name?" asked Naphtali, reaching out to touch the cat.

"No." The cat stared into space. "At least not yet. But if you want to know *who* I am, I'm a she-cat. You are familiar with Pessl the grocer at the north end of the village? My mother lives with him and my father belongs to the Rabbi's son. I myself reside between the two houses. However"—the cat now fixed her gaze on Naphtali—"however, now that spring has come, I spend my time exploring meadows. I've just discovered this apple tree. It's easy to climb and I adore the smell of appleblossoms." Her eyes were like flecked marbles. They caught the bright spring light.

"I adore appleblossoms, too. And so do my mother and my father. My brother Tobias is only eight months old, so he'd probably eat them if I put them near his nose."

The cat stretched, then opened her mouth in a huge yawn.

"More to the point, do they like *cats?* Your mother and father and Tobias who is only eight months old and eats whatever you put near his nose? Do they?"

Naphtali bit his bottom lip. Either this cat had been listening at Naphtali's window or she was very, very smart. He shook his head.

"My mother and I love cats. We both want a cat more than anything. I don't know what my baby brother Tobias loves more than anything, except milk. But my father just doesn't. He says, 'NO! No cat!' every time Mama and I ask him. And we ask him again and again. It's sad." Naphtali's mouth turned down.

The cat's ears twitched, then flattened.

"It is a pity! A pity! There was a time we cats were considered very special. As a matter of fact, with all due respect to God, yours and mine" — and she set to preening her tail — "the Egyptians thought we were divine. They put statues of cats in all their temples. They were the first to domesticate the cat in 2300 before the Christian era."

Naphtali was impressed. "All I know about the Egyptians is that they were very cruel to the Jews and made them slaves. And then Moses led them out of the land of Egypt and that's why we have Passover" — he stopped a moment to catch his breath — "which is coming this week." Naphtali paused, thinking: *Yes, he would ask her.*

"May I ask you something? May I give you a name? Would you mind?"

The cat opened and closed her eyes.

"Not at all. Actually I'd be most grateful, thank you. It is time I had a name. I can't answer to 'Cat' or a whistle forever. It's not dignified."

Naphtali was even more impressed. How well-spoken, how polite this cat was.

"I'd like to call you — Appleblossom."

The cat, who at that moment had been meticulously licking between her outspread toes, suddenly stopped short, one paw extended, rigid in the air, and looked up at Naphtali, puzzled.

"*Appleblossom? Appleblossom!* What kind of a name is that?"

Naphtali stroked the cat's ears and thought hard.

"I'll tell you what kind of a name it is. It's a name that will make something happen." He put his face against her side. "I don't know yet quite *how* it will happen, but I've a feeling." The cat was purring a hectic purr. It made Naphtali's face feel bumpy.

"Listen, Appleblossom." Naphtali smiled at the scraggly creature. "Listen. You need a home, isn't that right?"

The cat blinked her eyes into slits.

"And I want you to live with me. And I know my mother wants a cat, which means *she* wants you to live with us. Especially since she can fatten you up. And she loves appleblossoms and my father loves *her.* See?"

Naphtali pulled back from the cat, triumphant.

"See what?" Appleblossom gave a light jump over Naphtali's knees, turned, and sat up straight.

"See why I want to call you Appleblossom? You did come down from the apple tree and — "

There was a shout of voices. Naphtali jumped up and turned, glancing behind him.

"The other boys are here. The Rabbi will be opening the door now. I have to go." He grabbed his leather book strap. "I'll be back tomorrow. We'll think of a plan — maybe to go with Passover. And your name. It will be all right, Appleblossom. I know.

Don't go away, *please*," he called over his shoulder, bounding back down the path to the synagogue.

Appleblossom didn't stir. Her eyes were closed.

I'll be here, she purred to herself. *Oh, yes, Naphtali Ha-Levi, I'll be right here.*

"NO! NO CAT!" Naphtali's father wiped his mouth with a large blue-checkered napkin. He pushed his chair away from the table. "When Tobias is older, a bird perhaps . . ."

"But *why* don't you like cats, Papa?" Naphtali stood beside his father patting his hand.

"Naphtali!" His mother was holding Tobias to her breast. The baby nursed with one hand curled around her finger. "Naphtali, stop nagging your father. Papa doesn't like cats. It's a feeling he has. Just the way you and I love them, he doesn't."

"And," his father went over to the great tile stove in the middle of the room, "this is not the moment to bring an animal into the house. We've enough to do preparing for the holiday without an animal underfoot." He poured himself a cup of tea from the steaming samovar on the upper ledge. Then he sat down on the bench that encircled the stove.

Naphtali turned away. He knew how important it was to cleanse the house thoroughly for Passover. On Sunday he and his mother had scrubbed each piece of furniture. His father had washed down the walls and polished the windows till the glass fairly disappeared. And the morning of the Seder they would begin the final search to rid the house of every last crumb of bread and cake and cracker and cookie made with everyday flour and yeast leavening, just as they did each year.

What could Naphtali say? His father was a very wise man — in the village they called him a sage. Even the peasants came to consult him about their problems. If he said it was no time for a cat, well . . . But his heart was aching for the scruffy Appleblossom he'd left behind under the apple tree. Then he remembered Appleblossom's words concerning cats and Egyptians.

"Papa, the Egyptians *loved* cats. They 'mesticated them. They were the first."

Naphtali's father raised his eyebrows, which were very straight and thick. He turned to his wife.

"What is this Naphtali is saying? What about the Egyptians?"

Naphtali's mother smiled her brilliant smile. "Tell Papa what you mean, Naphtali. I *think* I know." She lifted Tobias to her shoulder. His head lay against her thick auburn hair.

Suddenly Naphtali's father put a hand to his head. "Wait, my love, wait. I know what he means. The Egyptians *do*-mesticated cats. Is that it, Naphtali?"

Naphtali gave a jump.

"Well, well." His father stretched out his long legs and unlaced his high shoes. "They may have treated their cats with affection, but they bound our people as slaves, forcing them to hard labor in the desert and forbidding them to practice their religion."

"That's what I told Apple . . . that's what I thought, Papa."

"Forget cats and remember Egypt." His father reached to take Tobias. "Thursday night is the first night of Passover, and all the family will be here. It's a busy time for us. There is still much to be done."

Naphtali's mother handed Tobias to her husband.

"I'll help Naphtali wash up. Then he can do his lessons and bring them to you."

Naphtali followed his mother into his bedroom. His featherbed against the wall was covered with a gaily colored quilt of flowered patches. Tobias slept in a cradle at the end of his parents' bed. In not too many months Naphtali knew he would be sharing his room with his brother. If only he could be sharing it with Appleblossom as well. If only . . .

Naphtali took off his shirt, and his mother squeezed out a soft yellow cloth into the washbasin on the dresser. It was soothing to have his face washed with her round, up-and-down strokes. She pushed his bangs back from his forehead, gave a long wipe across, and kissed his eyes — first one, then the other.

"What do I taste? Salt? Tears?" she asked gently.

"Oh, Mama." Naphtali threw his arms around his mother's neck.

She drew him close to her. "Don't worry so, Naphtali. Don't fret. Don't think about cats. Right *now*, don't think about cats. Study and learn. That's the most important business in your life. When Passover is over, we'll see. Yes" — and she nodded as if to assure herself — "*we will see about it.*"

Naphtali squirmed in his seat. The school day seemed endless. He looked at the clock. Finally the bell rang, and he was first out the door.

He raced down the cobblestone street toward the synagogue. He had to be sure that Appleblossom truly existed. His father called him a dreamer, and he knew he could dream away the hours. What if . . . ?

Appleblossom *was* there — not under the apple tree but on the steps of the synagogue.

"Appleblossom! Oh, Appleblossom, I was afraid —" Naphtali sat down beside his friend, catching his breath in loud, short gasps.

"You were afraid?" Appleblossom rubbed her chin against Naphtali's foot. "You thought I was merely a figment of your imagination? That I did not exist? Or perhaps that I did exist but that I had left the village in a huff?" She raised her back slowly till whatever bit of flesh she had rippled beneath her fur. Naphtali could see there was more bone than flesh. "Does the world really think," Appleblossom continued, "that only the dog is faithful? Evidently you are not familiar with a saying that goes, *A cat never leaves a home once it has chosen.* And I have chosen."

Naphtali took Appleblossom on his lap.

"I knew you would be here; at least part of me did." Naphtali hugged Appleblossom. "But the truth is, I was worried. 'Specially since I'd told you how Papa feels about cats." Naphtali took the cat's face in his hands. "But you *are* here and now we can make our plans."

Appleblossom angled out from Naphtali's hands and, with a graceful turn of her neck, began preening her tail.

"I'm giving it much thought, Naphtali Ha-Levi. Much deep thought." Suddenly she bounced away toward the meadow. "Here come the Rabbi and your other friends. I'll wait for you after class under the apple tree."

"Now," pronounced the Rabbi when the boys had settled down, "only two days till the first Seder. Therefore" — he put on his half-glasses and peered sharply at the class — "therefore, the youngest will recite the Four Questions."

Worn Haggadahs were eagerly opened. In their high voices the boys chanted: *"Mah nish-ta-nah, ha-lilah ha-zeh, mi-kol-ha-lay-lot?* Why is this night different from all other nights?"

Naphtali was not among the youngest, and by now he knew the questions by heart. He had been asking them at every Seder since he was four years old. His attention was focused instead on the open window. A long, slim branch of the largest chestnut tree in the village lay against the upper pane. It was just coming into flower. What *was* that object poised between two huge vertical blooms halfway along the bough? It wasn't white like the chestnut flowers. It wasn't a leaf. It was — Appleblossom! How light she must be. How —

"Naphtali Ha-Levi!" the Rabbi's voice thundered above the chanting. "Attention, please. ATTENTION."

The voices sang on. Naphtali could see the bough move ever so slightly. He forced his attention back to the Haggadah.

After the Four Questions the boys read the meaning of the Seder celebration. Finally they recited in unison the Kiddush, the blessing over wine, and then the blessing after the meal.

"After the third cup of wine is poured" — the Rabbi spoke most solemnly — "the door is opened for the prophet Elijah."

The branch on which Appleblossom was seated quivered, though there was no wind. Naphtali watched closely. Most definitely it had quivered.

The Rabbi took off his glasses, wiped them with his handkerchief, and put them into a large black metal case that shut with a snap. The lesson was over.

Tucking his Haggadah between his book straps, Naphtali bolted from the room.

By the time he reached the tree Appleblossom was there, lying in a patch of blue scilla that had opened overnight. Her eyes were slits. She looked as if she had been asleep for hours.

"Appleblossom —" Naphtali sat down crosslegged beside her — "were you listening to the class from that chestnut tree?"

"Of course I was listening. I've been listening for weeks," Appleblossom answered casually. "And thank goodness I have. And thank goodness the Rabbi went over the service so carefully. Otherwise I couldn't have come up with such a fine plan."

Naphtali jumped up. "You have a plan? Oh, Appleblossom, tell me. I've been thinking, too, but I haven't gotten very far. I just *know* if my father meets you and I tell him and my mother your name is Appleblossom and you came down from an apple tree and . . . Oh, tell me what you think we can do. Papa is *very* strong. He never goes back on his word. Never."

"Your Papa, so I've heard, is a very learned and religious man *and* a man of his word," Appleblossom agreed. "I promise you he will not have to go back on any word. That is in my plan. Only, I have to think it through a bit more."

"Appleblossom" — Naphtali was on his knees — "Appleblossom, I *do* love you." Then he was up and swinging his books and skipping all the way home.

Appleblossom sat and watched him go. She didn't move till Naphtali was out of sight. Then her ears twitched.

"You're a fine boy, Naphtali Ha-Levi. The plan will work. It *must* work."

17

After supper Naphtali's mother put a giant kettle of water on the stove. "I'm getting out the Passover dishes and the silverware. We'll wash them in boiling water and Papa will pass the pots through the fire to make everything pure for the holiday."

Naphtali's father climbed on a chair and opened the top doors of the great oak armoire in the corner of the kitchen. Down came the dishes Naphtali loved, with their flowing design of birds and flowers in rose and blue and gold dancing over the plates and around the edges of the cups and soup bowls. Down came the crystal wine goblets on straw-slim stems, rimmed with gold. Out of velvet-lined boxes came the knives and forks and spoons and salad forks and dessert spoons with raised flowers on the handles. How these treasures added to the excitement.

Naphtali's father had a faint smile on his lips as he handed down the pieces to his wife. A smile! *This would be an excellent moment*, Naphtali thought, and he tugged eagerly at his father's trousers.

"Papa, once a cat comes into the house, it never leaves. It's faithful. And you always tell me, be honest and be faithful. You always say that, Papa."

His father was off the chair and put an arm around Naphtali's shoulder. "You have a good mind for the Law, Naphtali. But I must tell you of another saying: *One can lose one's memory from patting a cat.* So why don't we just forget about cats." He looked into Naphtali's face. "Naphtali, you mustn't be sad. Passover is coming, the holiday of the escape from Egypt, the holiday of freedom, Naphtali. Of the Red Sea dividing so that our people might pass through. Of miracles, Naphtali. Here, give me a big smile."

Naphtali hid his face against his father's arm. He didn't feel like smiling. *Of miracles*, he repeated silently to himself. *Oh,*

Appleblossom, he thought, *I hope there's a real miracle in your plan. With Papa so set against having a cat, we're going to need one.*

Naphtali found Appleblossom ambling along the path from the stand of fruit trees. He picked her up and turned toward their apple tree. She was warm. She smelled as if she'd spent hours among the blossoms. The flowering tree was droning with bees. Gently he set the cat on the ground.

"There's no Hebrew school today. Tomorrow's Passover. Now you can tell me the plan and — my!" Naphtali stopped in the middle of his sentence. "Appleblossom, you look different. Shiny and . . . I don't know exactly. Just different."

Appleblossom passed her tongue over her right front paw and brought the paw to her cheek, brushing her fur upward.

"I've been preparing for my grand entrance."

"Your grand entrance? Tell me."

Appleblossom put forth each word the way Naphtali's father laid out the checkers on the board when he was about to play the last game — win or lose.

"What happens," asked the cat, "after the third cup of wine is blessed and drunk?"

"After the third cup?" Naphtali repeated. "You know, Appleblossom. You know the whole Seder by heart, I'll bet."

The cat purred in agreement. "Nevertheless, tell me."

"All right." Naphtali pulled in his chin and straightened up against the tree trunk. "The door is opened for the prophet Elijah to enter, if he should happen to be passing by. Of course, he" — Naphtali reached out and squeezed the cat so hard she nearly clawed free from his grasp — "is that it?"

"That's it!"

They stared at each other — four eyes wide with delight.

"You mean, when I open the door for Elijah — you walk in?"

"Almost," answered Appleblossom. "When Elijah comes in, I'll be right behind him. He won't mind. His soul is all kindness. He spends his life helping people, making them as happy as they can be. And your Papa, Naphtali, learned, pious man that he is, could never turn out a cat that is a companion of Elijah. And so . . ."

"But," Naphtali's sunny face was instantly all despair. "Appleblossom, Elijah doesn't *really* come. It's just that we *hope* he's there. That's why we set a chair for him and fill the large silver wine cup for him to drink. We have to be ready. But he never *really* comes."

Appleblossom looked up at the sky. "That's a point to ponder. Perhaps I will take it up with your father. We shall have many discussions on the fine points of the Law, I'm sure. So, how do you know Elijah doesn't *really* walk in? You must look harder, Naphtali. And trust me. He'll be there. And I'll be directly behind him. Then I shall be taken into your family and be loved and respected. And of course" — she snuggled against Naphtali's foot — "I shall love and respect all of you in return. And that will be that."

There was a long silence. Then Appleblossom added softly, "After all, Naphtali Ha-Levi, isn't that what learning is all about?"

Naphtali sat between his two grandfathers. His whole body still tingled from the scrub his mother had given him hours before.

"Everything and everybody has to be scoured to a new brightness for this holiday," she had told him, as she did every year. Now she looked proudly across the table at her elder son. Papa, in the long white robe he wore only on the most sacred occasions, reclined in a chair piled high with pillows. On either side sat Naphtali's grandmothers. There were aunts and uncles and cousins, but no other young children.

"I wish Uncle Aaron and Aunt Miriam could be here," Naphtali's mother announced to the assembled guests.

"They're probably making a Seder with Aaron's family. Where is it?" Naphtali's father asked.

"In the center of America — in Chicago," an uncle answered. "Even in America Jews manage to bake matzo and make hard-boiled eggs." Everyone laughed.

At the far end of the table sat his parents' best friends, Cyrille and Dov. "They have no children, Naphtali," his father had explained, "and we Jews believe that at Passover no one should sit at a table without children. No matter how much wealth a man has, if he has no children, he is a poor man."

And if a child has no cat, he is a poor child, Naphtali had added, but only in his head.

"Everything is beautiful." Both grandmothers clapped their hands.

"My daughter-in-law is the best of wives." Grandmother Ha-Levi threw a kiss to Naphtali's mother.

"And a splendid mother," added Grandmother Brody with pride.

The table was a lovely sight. A deep glass bowl held apple-blossoms that scented the whole room. On each side of the bowl stood tall candlesticks with their short white holiday candles. The plates of matzo were covered with snowy white napkins. And everywhere the birds and flowers in blue and rose and gold flew over the white tablecloth, shimmering in a breeze, or so it seemed to Naphtali.

Beside Naphtali's father was a cut-glass decanter filled with deep-red wine. Elijah's cup glowed in the candlelight.

And then it was time.

Naphtali recited the Four Questions in a clear, steady voice, though in his chest his heart was beating even faster than when he had raced down the path looking for Appleblossom. *What would happen?* his heart beat out. *What would happen?*

The dinner, all agreed, was the finest ever prepared. Naphtali's mother grew rosy with the compliments. Tobias in his cradle lay content, clutching a rattle.

Suddenly the glasses were being filled for the third time and Naphtali's father was saying, "Open the door, Naphtali, that the prophet Elijah may enter our home on this holy night."

Naphtali slid off his cushioned chair and opened the door. His legs felt like jelly. His grandfathers began chanting.

"Praise the Lord, all ye nations,
Laud Him, all ye peoples,
For His mercy is great toward us
And the truth of the Lord endureth forever. Hallelujah!"

At the conclusion of these words, in through the open door came Appleblossom, head and tail held high, skinny little body sleek and immaculate. She looked neither to the right nor to the left. She walked across the room and lay down beside Naphtali's father's chair.

Everyone stared. No one said a word. Grandmother Brody clapped a handkerchief to her mouth.

Naphtali's mother glanced at his father with a look halfway between a question and a decision. His father was staring down at the cat, who lay comfortably with eyes shut.

His father then looked from the cat to his wife, to the chair set out for Elijah, to Elijah's cup. Naphtali followed his father's eyes. Not a word had been spoken.

Ever so slowly, Naphtali's father shook his head and closed his eyes. Naphtali held his breath.

Suddenly there was a strange sound. A most unusual sound. *His father was chuckling!* Naphtali had seen him smile, had heard him laugh. But Papa never chuckled. And there he was—chuckling! Little wrinkles appeared at the corners of his eyes and lips. Reaching down, with a single finger he stroked the cat's back.

"Well, well, a cat," he said.

"Her name is Appleblossom, Papa," Naphtali whispered, knowing that the miracle had taken place. "*Appleblossom.*"

The illustrations in this book were done in radiant watercolors
and pencil on Fabriano Hot Press 140-lb. paper.
The borders were done on Esdee scratchboard.
The display type was set in Nicholas Cochin.
The text type was set in Cochin.
Calligraphy by Judythe Sieck
Composition by Thompson Type, San Diego, California
Color separations were made by Bright Arts, Ltd., Singapore.
Printed and bound by Tien Wah Press, Singapore
Production supervision by Warren Wallerstein and Michele Green
Designed by Michael Farmer
Edited by Jane Yolen